BESIDE THE BROOK

A COLLECTION OF SHORT STORIES

LALITA VAITHEESWARAN

ISBN 979-888555679-8

Contents

Contents

Acknowledgements

My abundant gratitude to my family who is the reason, and the force, behind my venture.
My thankfulness to my friends for their constant support and encouragement.
I shall remain ever grateful for the bountiful benevolence of the Almighty.
I am extremely grateful to unsplash.com for all the images used in this book.
My gratitude to Notion Press for publishing this book.

Preface

About the Book

Stories spring from experiences and reality. They weave in them, threads of vehemence, humor or learning. The book is a collection of short stories of varied genres which evoke a myriad of emotions.The pandemic and the ensuing hardships, due to loss of livelihood, has been picturised in some of the stories.

About the Author

Lalita Vaitheeswaran is a gynecologist having a passion for writing in both Hindi and English.

She has authored 3 books of poetry and is part of many anthologies across the globe.

She has been the recipient of many awards and accolades for her writing ventures.

1
Beauty of Nature

It was a great day for Adil Dossabhoy, the renowned builder and developer. He had been awarded the tender for developing Mayura forests in the outskirts of Bangalore.

Everywhere across the length and breadth of the country were his projects ringing in modernity, ease and splendid architecture.

Navroz Malls, Navroz Stadium, Navroz Towers- each one spelt swankiness and style.

Mayura forests was the thousand-acre dense forest belt connecting the main city with Ramnagaram and Krishnakuti, the small villages in and around Bangalore. People cheered and applauded as now the villages would have a better connection with the main city.

Adil set off in his chauffeured Mercedes, settling on its rear seat trying to ease himself

from the sweltering heat outside and exhaustion from the string of endless meetings he had been engaged in for winning this project. With his laptop plugged in and head phones he was busy calculating the nitty- gritty of the business deal.

A mild headache had already started to nag him and while he tried his best to divert himself, he felt uneasy. He asked the chauffer Manish. the exact location, which seemed miles away. Manish suggested that they could take a small break at the opening of the forest where the green meadows and the canopy of trees

were leading into the dense timberland.

Adil alighted and walked towards the teak and Sandal trees. A cuckoo started singing on the branches just over him.

A beautiful aromatic breeze laden with freshness began stirring his soul.

He could hear the gurgling of a stream and he started walking in its search only to find a gush of pure water flowing over colourful pebbles. Wild flowers of every colour adorned the swampy land around and he almost ran to catch a butterfly! Chirping and fluttering birds seemed to be tale telling the angst of the woods. Owls hooted and leaves rustled in the wind which whispered and whistled through the branches. A wandering cloud like snow beckoned to take him to the skies........... He was melting...he did not know what was overcoming on his own self.

He took giant steps towards his car,

And typed on his laptop to those concerned.

Mayura forests are going to become the abode of only the beautiful nature. I refuse to meddle or peddle to turn the paradise into another human woe!

2

A Flicker of Hope

It was well past two months. Pundit Ramnath who was the only priest performing all rituals had lost his earnings due to the pandemic.The village Shyampur was surrounded by such many small villages which witnessed many pujas, festivals, celebrations , weddings and even last rites, was now deserted as no one dared to come out of their houses.

" Where is the *dal* today?" Asked punditji

" Its over...and theres no money for more" wife Rukmani was almost in tears.

The last month had been frugal and the vegetables had already vanished from their meals....

" At least we never used to buy cereals and vegetables till this doomed disease made its appearance....our *yajmans* used to bless us with all these..."Rukmani was reminiscing....

Now it's all over....no pujas means no money....and the end of life for us....she shuddered as she spoke.

Their children were inconsolable .

"Amma I want more dal !"

"Sorry children....we will get it soon...dont worry...oh God ! Please help"...and she started chanting the *shlokas* which she always did for mental strength.

HOPE

"Hey Shambhu ! Isnt it your father's death anniversary tomorrow?" Pundit Ramnath was hopeful to get some earnings....

" It is......but I'm wary of doing it at home...Its wise not to call many people home......so I'm not doing it this time..." Shambhu was a little curt.

Pundit Ramnath was thinking...."Oh couldn't he have given me some *dakshina?*"

No way out....theres no way out of this poverty.....God please help...." and he also started chanting the *Hanuman Chaalisa*.....

************.

Many people were returning to their villages as there was a massive lay off in other cities.

Aman, their neighbour's brother also returned from Delhi.He had been working as a contractor in a small company which had now closed.

"Punditji....*Pranam*....how are you doing..." he smiled as he removed his heavy bag from his shoulder...

Punditji could only hide his sorrow with difficulty...

"How are you Aman...and what would you do now?"Punditji was concerned about the job losses ..

Aman chuckled...

"I'm in search of a job...am browsing the net for that...."

Punditji was amazed to see the internet and know about it.

Aman showed him how he was talking to his Delhi contacts through video chats....

And then he suddenly turned to him......

"Punditji.....Why dont you use the internet and do your pujas for your *yajmans?*

You can ask them to pay you through the phone also.

You can do mass rituals of "*tarpan*" on "*Amavasya*" days and even if you collect Rs. fifty from each you will have a good amount...."

Punditji's eyes beamed with joy and surprise ......

A flicker of hope crossed his gaze as he made plans to buy a smart phone with internet connections.

At last,.... there would be old days again when children would have full stomachs.

Glossary

Tarpan : A ritual performed on new moon for ancestors

Dakshina: Donation

Yajmans : host

Amavasya: New moon

3
The Haunted House

It was well past midnight.I was driving through deserted roads as usual, as part of my work compulsions, when it started to drizzle.The wipers made frightening rhythmic noises. I was already chanting my prayers in fear as I maneuvered through shadows of trees skirting the road which looked like ghosts.The eerie silence was suddenly broken by my ringing phone when I almost jumped with fear.

Ms Shefali ?" said a mysterious voice..

Who is this? I tried to hide my fear and thundered...

A moan... and he hung up..

The car started to squeal,grind as it stopped to a screeching halt.As I figured out where I was, I recognised the familiar Banyan tree.Just next was the rumoured palatial house which was single and stood alone overlooking a small pond.

My heart raced and thumped as I was sure to be devoured by the ghosts of the haunted house.As I got out of the car to open the bonnet to see what went wrong I could hear rattling sounds from inside..A pale, ashen, cadaverous structure started walking towards me...It was a shapeless figure signalling to me with hands.I shouted for help and my voice was lost in wilderness.

Suddenly a black cat jumped out of nowhere ..Its shining eyes stared at me..meow...and it jumped across to vanish in the dark..A large spider with gleaming big eyes stared at me.....I could see lizards

as big as crocodiles and as they opened their large mouths to gobble me I swiftly jumped to the other side.

I could hear the tinkling of anklets and clanging of bangles...amidst the swoosh of the wild breeze.

I gathered all my wit and grit and shouted...

Who are you?

What do you want...?

The shadowy torso started walking towards me and as I got ready to scramble my way to run, I was shocked as the silhouette now ensembled as a beautiful new bride ...she was conscious and dreamy eyed as though still in the effect of sedation...while she stammered and lisped ....

"Please help...Im not a ghost....."

I was astounded...and called up the emergency helpline number.

In no time there were sirens and beacon lights surrounding the house...

The woman was quickly taken on a stretcher...and shifted to the hospital...

Horror greeted us when there were many such women inside, all shackled and chained...being held captive in a house which was wilfully rumoured to be haunted to aid in such immoral and illegal activities...

The police thanked me and applauded my courage while I was proud to be able to bust not only a crime but also a superstition.

4
The Accident

The small five year old child was brought by locals to the hospital bleeding and unconscious They said she was apparently the only survivor of the accident in which a tourist bus had fallen into a deep gorge 20 kms away.Sister Molly,the nurse, had been the incharge of the Paediatric ICU for 15 years and was considered the most competent of all the paramedics.She had the astute skills of an eagle along with a warm heart.

The small child was angelic...with her black curls and dark eyes..

We named her "**Mili**" as we had found her!

Thankfully and miraculously Mili had no major problems as her investigations revealed.

It was also the continuous and unstinted labour of Sister Molly that had shown results.Molly had got deeply and emotionally attached to Mili and looked after her day and night like her own mother.

On the second day, Mili started opening her eyes and crying shouting for her mom...It was a heart wrenching scene...

The police arrived with the 'Women and Child Welfare' president Mrs Anandi Bose..and declared that once the baby recovers she has to be shifted to a welfare home as she had lost her parents in the accident.

Molly was incosolable...her swollen eyes showed her love and bond she had developed for Mili.

"Ma'am...please...do not separate her from me...I wont be able to live without her".. she cried .

Molly, as everyone knew, was childless and was hoping to adopt a baby but was fed up of the long procedures.

We were all in tears...and urged Mrs Bose to help.During the week she spoke to the police commissioner and other adoption authorities.

****

A car screeched to a halt...and Mrs Bose stepped out with some papers...

Molly was asked to sign on them.

And was handed Mili.

As Molly cuddled the child...Mili shouted *Mumma*....

Eveveryone was teary eyed and was clapping away in glee!

5

The Ring

The old age home was decorated with festoons and balloons. The inmates ran hither and thither to make the celebration memorable...

I was there as their general physician to do their monthly health check-up.

"Dr Sneha...please stay back and be our honourable guest today"...they pleaded.....and I agreed.

I have been visiting this place for the last some months. Surekha *tai* as everyone called her was the most loved inmate. She was around 60 years but age defied her and she still looked beautiful. Tall with sharp features her big bindi stood out and she would tie her long hair in a bun.

After losing her husband her son now in US had shifted her into this home as he could not come home frequently.

Surekha *tai* was looking ravishing today.Dressed in a blue paithani zari saree...she would make any new bride run for her money.

She was blushing and acted coy...as she reminisced on her memories of youth.

****

Dattatray used to be at the same bus stop as she ..and would never cease to take a secret gaze at her lovingly.Though Surekha was aware of this she wouldn't respond for fear of the society.

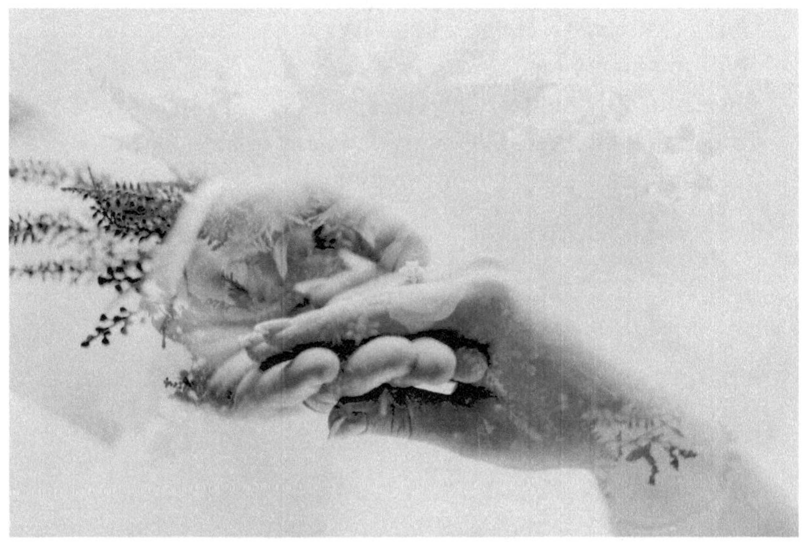

After somedays he gathered the courage to come to her and propose to her with a gold ring.

Surekha was too scared to even speak. Though she too had developed feelings for him she was not sure if her family would even think of a "love marriage" happening !

And she did not want to disrespect her family nor did she want to hurt his feelings.

She changed her bus stop.

Years rolled on...She got married...and had a fulfilling life. Her son was settled in US but her husband died of a heart attack.

Here, Dattatray remained a bachelor...he could never think of anyone else..

His ageing compelled him to come to an old age home.

That day when he arrived....he saw Surekha.

Their eyes met.

Instantly they recognized each other.

Old feelings rejuvenated for each other and upon exchanging their stories......they became closer by hearts...

He showed her the same gold ring.
"Kaay..tu.majhyasi..lagna...karsheel...ka?"
(Will you marry me?)
She could only mutter..."*hoy*"..(Yes)
I stood there with tears flowing down my eyes..
Watching the amazing ring ceremony !

6

Our Frontline Heroes

Sakharam was teary eyed while he collected the hospital waste and carried it to the sanitation department.His pregnant wife was due for delivery in another week but he wasn't able to go as he wasn't given leave.

Dr Rahul Sharma, the ICCU physician read his eyes and went to him clad in his PPE braving the deluge of Covid patients.

Sakharam! dont worry. We are all in the same boat. Tell me her whereabouts so that I tell my colleague there to tend to her.

Thank you *Sahab*...Sakharam could not stop his tears..

Suddenly there was chaos.

Two policemen were wheeled into the emergency. Constable Mahipal was bleeding as he had been run over by curfew violators.Sub Inspector Rohit was wincing in pain as his hand had been crushed by rioters.They were taken into the Operation theatre and were being clinically assessed for surgery by Dr Rahul.

"Doctor *sahab*...please save me. You are God."

Prayed the policemen.

Dr Rahul smiled and patted them softly.

You are our heroes...Nothing will happen to you..just stay calm.

Sister Angela came running with IV fluids and antibiotics and as she put in the IV line she prayed to God for their well being.

Sir..Madam is on the line...she said to Dr Rahul...as she put the phone to his ears.

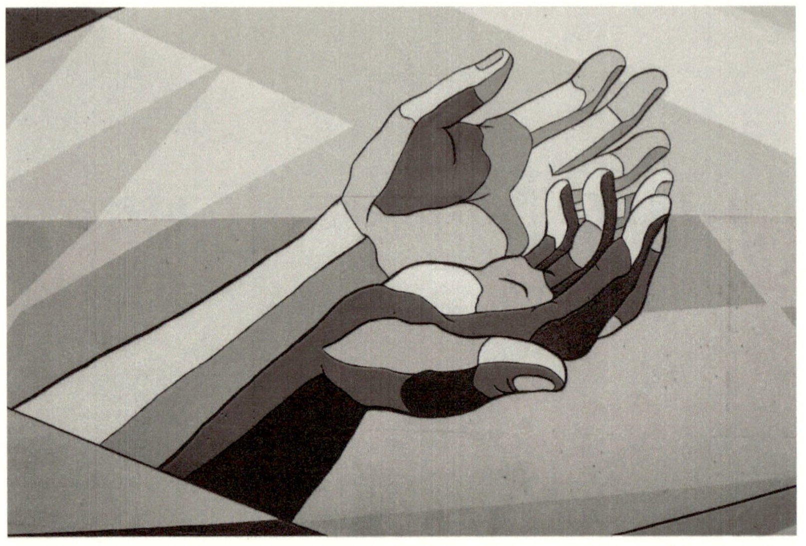

As he listened...he looked stone faced and numb.

It wasn't the wife...it was the CMO of the district hospital.

Dr Rahul ! your wife Dr Sudha has to be taken in isolation...as a patient in her ward has tested positive.

Sir...but my five year old daughter...cant stay alone...and I cant leave my hospital...he begged as he cried.

Dont worry doc...I am also your friend....she will be taken care of in our hospital nursery.

Sister Angela was praying.

Oh God !

First Sakharam...then the policemen..and now our favourite Dr Rahul's wife..Please keep them safe...

.

.

I was sipping my tea as the delivery boy rang my doorbell to deliver my essentials.....I thanked him profusely as I pledged to do MY least...

To stay home !

7
Memories of Summers past

Bhola and his family had just returned to their native village as the urban cities came to a standstill .Life's uncertainties and desperation stared at them. Maya his wife and three children were inconsolable. As they settled in a small mud house which they called their own, they looked at the parched fields and despondent looks of neighbours.

"How beautiful was the last summer!" Maya uttered amidst hiccups and tears...You could sell all mangoes and vegetables and I my earthen pots.

The contractor Bhatia sahab was so nice that he would give us some litchis and bananas for our Munna...

Remember how when we first drank that chilled lassi?

Oooh it was heavenly!

I had saved some money to buy a table fan this year....and now all our money has gone...Bhola choked as he was listening silently to his wife's woes which wouldn't seem to end..

She was going on and on reminiscing.

How children enjoyed the merry go round and even the giant wheel at the weekly market .

Look...that sari I could get for 200 rupees...is still so beautiful.

Baba baba...cried the seven year old Shiva.. as he was scratching his sweaty back which had developed rashes... I want those days again....I could get beautiful clothes from those flat owners across the road.

Ma!....called Geeta, who was around ten.....summers were so nice there when baba got us those kulfies...and remember how one gentleman got us some food on his son's birthday?

We want those days back...sobbed the youngest child Suman of only five....summers full of swings, and panna stalls from generous people..

Will we ever go back?

Or these will remain memories of our best summers?

The children couldn't be calmed.

even as both Bhola and Maya tried their best to pacify them.

Some memories are etched in the mind...they sighed...as they went on to smear their new fireplace or *'chulha'* with cowdung.

Both the *chulha* and their hearts were burning.

8

Happy Halloween....

It was a beautiful evening . The whole city was still decorated with lights even though the festival was over.I was travelling by a cab to attend my friend Smith's birthday bash in a farmhouse in the outskirts of Timba, around two hours from where I lived.Carefully holding the bouquet lest it should get withered I was enjoying the scene from my window as the car sped on the expressway overtaking many.The cabbie struck a conversation with me.He was a frail looking man with mysterious looks.He started describing every building we crossed, its history and how it got its name.It was getting foggy and darker as we travelled and soon a drizzle began.The wiper of the cab with its rhythmic sound was making the travel a little creepy.

The driver started music on his radio to keep up the chirpiness but my mind was restless. I wanted to reach my friend as soon as possible. Suddenly the car started swaying only to stop suddenly with a screech.

It's the tyre... sighed the driver...

Sir..we would have to seek help as I don't have the necessary equipment...

The drizzle was almost gone and so we both got out of the car and started looking for help.

*There...that...*he pointed to a house. *At the end of the street....*

As we started to move...

There was a big scream. ..and something hit my face...All I could see was many skeletons walking , running, laughing and even talking...

I started losing my consciousness...my heart raced..but I couldnt shout....I ..I ...had lost my voice...

The cabbie ...where was he?. And I saw him....as the same skeleton...smiling at me...saying...

Welcome to the haunted house....

Many skeletons walked towards me...with flowers. Sweets...and drinks...

I was.....perspiring ...gasping but not able to speak a word ......

And..

Suddenly ....

All lights were lit...

And someone called me...Hey William! This is Smith.

And all others came out laughing...

Happy Halloween....

Welcome to Smith's Birthday Bash...

I just fainted.....

And...

Am writing this from the hospital...

9
My child and I

The rummy party was bustling with merriment as the ladies dealt and distributed the cards.

Mrs Rita Bakshi, the host was in her pink gossamer best as she put the small infant in the cradle.

Mrs Bajaj, Mrs Ghosh,Mrs Arora,Mrs Sharma ..all the guests envied Rita who had the best vital statistics even as she became a mom recently.

Bindiya,the help was running hither and thither carrying short-eats and soft drinks to the guests.

As she passed the cradle, her longing loving eyes for the baby could not be hidden from the sharp eyes of Mrs Ghosh.

Rita! beware! She whispered...

Your maid is setting her eyes on your angel...

Rita just laughed and let go...

Such small parties were a regular affair at Rita's.

Bindiya would be seen cleaning, and decorating the hall and also preparing lip smacking snacks.

She would not miss her cooing and petting the baby at all times.

Every day she would overhear the grand ladies whispering and nudging asking Rita to be cautious of her.

On that day it was the child's first birthday. She was dressed up like a doll and her light angelic eyes lit up the ambience.

Bindiya couldn't control herself as she rushed to smear her forehead with a little kohl from her eyes.

That was enough for Mrs Ghosh...who sprang to catch Bindiya by her arm and intimidate her with her stare.

Rita came in and joined the melee'...

How dare you...how dare you put that black spot on my baby? The room echoed with her thundering query.

Bindiya's lacrymal glands gave in to a deluge of tears...

And she stammered but asserted....

Who am I ?

I AM THE(biological) MOTHER

AND SHE IS MY CHILD..

Dont forget that I made you a mother by surrogacy...you can physically take my baby but cannot cut the emotional umbilical cord!

Can't I ward off evil spirits from my own baby?I have never wanted anything more except that I could see my baby growing.....

The guests were flabbergasted as they listened to an emotional mother.....and they started dispersing from the party without eating....

10

My Heart Says: Professional Ethics is Supreme

As Dr. Pallavi sat on her desk sipping coffee she was sweating, and lost in thoughts.

"Was I right or wrong?"

She had a wedding invitation in her hand

Deeya weds Aniket

****

Her thoughts took her back two years ago...

****

There had landed an emergency case in her hospital...

The girl in her late twenties was unconscious ; her pulse very feeble.

Both her colleague Dr Shobhit , a surgeon and she simultaneously mumbled,

"Ectopic pregnancy..."

The girl was quickly wheeled into the operation theatre and was being prepared for surgery.

As soon as Dr. Pallavi looked at her, she was shocked!

The patient was Deeya, a family acquaintance's daughter. Though Deeya did not know Dr. Pallavi, the latter knew her very

well through the group

photographs circulated in social media groups.

There was a young man with her in his late 20s who was the only accompanying person...who looked visibly shaken...

He, while signing on the consent form told them he was Arun,her boyfriend, and that they were going to get married soon.

The surgery was successful and Deeya was discharged in two days.

Dr. Pallavi had sleepless nights and on top of that she was not in a position to confide in anyone....not even the husband...

Days rolled on.

****

A year passed.

Dr.Pallavi had gradually come over that incident.

There was a small commotion at the hospital reception.

"Ma'am Dr. Mallika your colleague wants to meet you..." Reeta,the receptionist phoned her in her chamber.

" Ooh..send her in "

Dr. Mallika was a radiologist, and her son, a very promising engineer, was the most eligible bachelor of the city.

After the niceties,

Mallika continued.

" Actually...we have almost finalized my son Aniket's marriage. The girl is Deeya. Since you know their family I thought it would be the best to ask you about her.I actually have heard some rumours that she had been admitted to your hospital for an abortion....please...please...tell me...as it is my son's future..."

Dr.Pallavi was taken aback.

She was in the so called *"Dharmsankat"* which *Arjuna* in *Mahabharat* was facing...

Keeping her face straight...calm and emotionless...

She answered...

"SORRY Mallika....I know the family but don't know intimate details of the girl.

As for the rumour of any abortion....It must be a rumour as I don't know of anything happening in my hospital...."saying this she excused herself and left...

She drove back home, dashed into her bedroom and cried...

Lying is a sin...

But..

Disclosing a professional secret would be a breach of trust between a doctor and the patient who completely trusts the former.

Yes...she had her answer.

My heart says...Professional ethics is supreme.

Wiping her tears, she was ready to have her cuppa.

11

Traffic Jam

"Here..yes here..put the flower garlands here.." Mahesh *mama* was ordering the florists..

"And the festoons and bulbs are to be put in this manner.." he was showing them some catalogues and pamphlets..

"*Bhaiyya* Have you told the caterers to add ras malai instead of rabdi..." panted Shobha *bua.*

" Here keep these bangles and necklace safely with you Guddi..." Mrs. Saxena was giving the ornaments to *Mami*...While Mr. Saxena was busy checking some accounts...

There was hustle bustle everywhere as the auspicious occasion of " Baarat" of the beautiful Megha was nearing..

She looked stunning in her dark red lehenga studded with embellishments...and the glow on her face revealed how eager she was to enter into wedlock with her childhood friend Ritesh....

Sahil *chacha* was busy coordinating with the *baratis* and guiding them to the venue which had been selected by the would be couple,lovingly.

Only that it was on one end of the city almost in the outskirts.

The *muhurat* was approaching and the *Punditji* started calling out for the families...

Here Sahil chacha's face was evidently showing all the anxiousness....and he could be seen sweating...

"What happened Sahil?" Asked Mr. Saxena...and his enthusiasm started to turn into panic..

"The Barat is caught in a traffic jam"...Sahil *chacha's* voice was quivering...

Call the *var.. vadhu* ...fast...the *Punditji* kept repeating..

The whole family seemed to now gather into a huddle and looked for options...

Megha was almost in tears...and feared that the selected auspicious *muhurat* would go in vain...

Suddenly she got a video call from Ritesh...

He showed her how his car was stuck in a serpentine queue of vehicles and any venture coming out looked futile!!

"Now what Ritesh...what...?" Megha was inconsolable..

Wait! wait..I have an idea"...Ritesh chuckled..."I am a techie....shall put technology into our marriage instead of fireworks....

Lets have an *e wedding*.....Call Punditji and everyone else..."

The newspapers were rife the next day

With the headlines :

The traffic jam wedding was as sweet as the pudding!

12

Justice

The court room was jam-packed. Everyone wanted to be witness to today's peculiar case and all eyes were on the Judge Justice Sunil Mehta. The defendant was the son of the well-known business tycoon Akash Malhotra who had been accused of siring the offspring of the plaintiff Neha who was now demanding that she be given half of his property.

Media was rife with allegations and counter allegations and channels increased their TRPs with their decibels and debates.

The attorney of Neha was vociferous and as he held the DNA report as testimony, all held their breath and dropped their jaws staring wide.

Akash Malhotra is now finished .. they exclaimed.

"Order order"....said the judge..

As he called upon the attorney of the defendant, Deepak Chopra,to cross examine and question .

"Where was your child born?" Advocate Deepak Chopra asked...

"Goodwill fertility clinic" responded Neha.

"Aaah..." said the lawyer...was it a normal delivery or a case of Artificial Reproductive technique(ART)?"

Even before Neha could say softly..ART...

Advocate Deepak Chopra tore into her answers...

What was the technique?

Was it IVF?....

"No"....she was getting more defensive..."it was artificial insemination..."

"H or D?"....he roared...

"I repeat.....

Was it husband ...or Donor...?"

And everything seemed to fall flat...

Akash Malhotra's son had once donated his sperms in this very clinic whose lab in charge was the brother of an ex-employee of Akash who had been fired.

And his sperms had been used as an ART for Neha.

Even though sperm banks do not disclose or leak the donors' names...he had conspired with Neha, to not only malign Akash Malhotra but also to loot him.

Justice Sunil Mehta was ready with his verdict...

Akash Malhotra's son was innocent.

Neha, her husband, the sperm bank manager and his brother were all booked for criminal conspiracy.

Justice was delivered!

13
The Burning Planet

I ran to Jumman chacha's shop.I was already panting.

"Chacha please give me 2 bottles of air and 4 bottles of water."

Chacha looked at me with dismay and his eyes rolled

"Whatttt?? 2 more bottles of air?? You have already taken 2 bottles this month and if you know the law you cannot get more than 3 bottles a month !!"

I began to plead..."Chacha please.....Maa has severe cough this time.she needs bottled air the Doctor has said...or else the polluted atmospheric air would further go to her lungs to destroy them..she has already used my quota as I was breathing well ...."

.."Only this time ..ok??...no more bottles...If the mayor comes to know..he would blacklist me..."

"Ok ok chacha...thank you..."

I stacked 2 bottles of air and 4 bottles of water and started running home.....

Aye.. listen.....aye....

I was startled to hear that thundering voice . .I knew it was Bhojraj the goon...notorious for "air snatching"

I hid my 2 bottles behind the dupatta and started walking as if I didnt hear him...

"What are you hiding?"...he thundered...."And if it is air...just hand it over quietly....or Ill kill you....."....he flaunted a knife...

" Bhaiyya.....plll..pl...please....let me go.....its for my maa....shes coughing like hell...All Doctors have just given a common medicine..
" clean air"..
Bhaiyya...please...

Suddenly the siren of a police vehicle was nearing.....

I heaved a sigh of relief ...and Bhojraj started retreating....

I fled for my life holding the air bottles close .....no I cant lose them....noway....!!

The streets were full ofadvertisements...of

Air Banks

Air lockers

Air investment

Air harvesting

..

..

..

And I could hear my son ....

Mumma...get up....Ill be late for school...

.....

I was sweating profusely....Yes I was breathing normally...

The air

Not from bottles...but from around...

Thank God...but the nightmare could turn true if I'm not careful.

14
Across the Burma Bridge

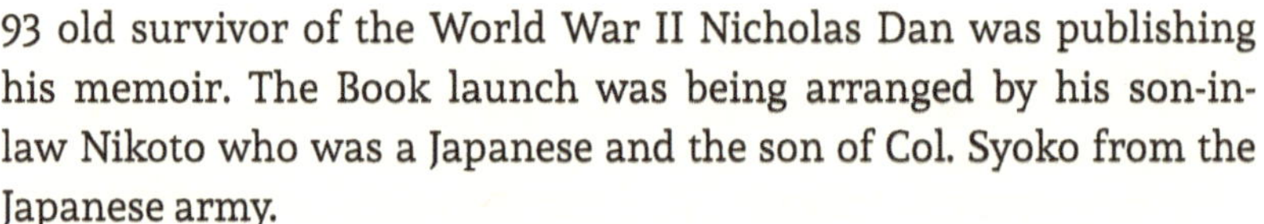

93 old survivor of the World War II Nicholas Dan was publishing his memoir. The Book launch was being arranged by his son-in-law Nikoto who was a Japanese and the son of Col. Syoko from the Japanese army.

*****

Young Nicholas who was part of the British army, was bidding adieu to his beautiful wife Sandra and daughter Carol, as he had been called to fight in the Burma campaign where the allied forces were facing the giant Japanese troops. Col.Syoko was second in command of the regiment under Maj.Gen.Myoto and was spearheading the battle, with loss of lives on both sides. Nicholas, along with his troop was captured and made POW (Prisoner of war) in the difficult terrains of Burma.

A surge of POWs was seen entering Burma as tough Japanese forces were compelling handcuffed and shackled men to build a bridge across the river Kwai. They were being pushed, kicked, and made to work.

Nicholas suddenly felt weak and nauseous. He was vomiting and fell unconscious. Major General Myoto kicked him on the abdomen,

You Good for nothing

and threw him in the dark jungles to perish.

Col. Syoko was watching this from a distance. As soon as his senior vanished from view, Syoko ran into the jungle. He made

Nicholas sit up and took out medicines from his pocket. He gave him water to drink and ensured that Nicholas felt better.

Nicholas was a true army man. He recoiled back into action and walked towards the construction site and help making the bridge. His eyes melted as he thanked Profusely Col. Syoko and the Lord. Cases of such torture of POWs became a regular sight. The Japanese were ferociously cruel, never hesitating to kick on the person of any prisoner who was unwell, had ulcers or had diarrhea. Nicholas was privy to these torments and had developed a hatred for the Japanese.

When Col. Myoto would leave after much abusing, a soft Col.Syoko would go around checking on the prisoners on the sly, giving them water or medicines and praying for them. He even told Nicholas once that had he not been part of the duty-bound Japanese army, he would never have been a party to this cruel, ghastly work. Nicholas has tears rolling down his cheeks as he reversed his general opinion about the Japanese.

****

Back home, Sandra and Carol received a mail from the British Army about Nicholas's capture. They were asked to help their respective troops in whichever way they could while at the same time not to befriend anyone from the enemy as

Loose lips might sink ships

A year had passed with no news of Nicholas's well-being, when suddenly they were startled to see him arriving home. He narrated how Col.Syoko helped him survive those tough days of torture and how he helped him escape unhurt.

******

Ten years later.

Father Xavier is reading out the marriage vows,

Both Carol and Nikoto say

I do!

15
Youthful Adventures

"Happy Birthday Sam!" Abhilash, his bestie was more than excited.

"Hey thanks buddy" chirped Samarth, aka Sam. "Just look out of the window"

As Abhilash pushed the curtains to see outside, a brand-new red Mercedes was parked and Sam was

swirling the keys from the driver's seat!

"By Jove! What a gift!! Only last year you had got that Audi?"

"Oh ...she's grown pretty old now!"

"Come fast for a drive"

"Wait! Let me carry our stuff chum' winked Abhi as he hurried into his room.

Both Sam and Abhi were childhood friends as both their parents were amongst the who's who of the city. Owners of immense wealth and possessions, they were exploring and wanting to taste newer experiences daily.

"What's this youth for, if one does not adventure" was their favorite quote.

Abhi came out with a backpack stuffed with snacks, cigarettes and liquor.

Both of them set out as they smiled impishly, pressing the accelerators hard.

Pandit Naresh Upadhyay adjusted his dhoti as he entered the principal's room.

"Yes Punditji come in, said Mr. Shyam Gupta, the principal

"I got your letter about the activities. A two-day camping in Dhamera is a good idea. You have been the force behind the library, the football court and indoor games in our school."

"Sir I want the youth to sweat it out. They are a bundle of energy which they need to channelize in a positive way so that they're focused and don't go astray."

Punditji was planning to show the boys river rafting, trekking, nature walks and minimalism. He asked the boys to be ready early morning the next day.

"There would be strict discipline followed and anyone flouting the rules penalized." Punditji announced

Punditji's own son Raghuveer was also part of the camp.

Dhamera was a small town on the banks of the river Ganges in the foothills of the mountains. The boys were overjoyed as a short three-hour bus journey would take them to an exciting experience for lifetime.

The bus halted at the stop. The boys got down one by one. Punditji was the last to come out.

As they had to go to the other side of the road, Pundit ji asked the boys to fall in a line and be very careful while crossing.

As the disciplined queue of boys crossed, there was a screech, and an over-speeding brand new red Mercedes hit and ran over Punditji who gasped and breathed his last.

The newspapers screamed the next day

"Do today's youthful adventurers also include killing the innocents?"

16
Hiroshima

Dr. Davis Alfred could not sleep that night. He had scanned two patients with similar defects in their baby in-utero. The head of the baby was smaller than normal and both the limbs had a deformity. He was waiting for dusk so that he could talk to his colleague Dr Sairo Yakamto who was a renowned oncologist in thwhole of Hiroshima, the island city of Honshu

"How can this be true?" Dr. Sairo was almost muttering to himself.

Dr. Davis showed him the scans while both had a cup of black coffee and sandwiches as they discussed the medical reports.

"Mutations!" exclaimed Dr Sairo as he came to a conclusion. It had been almost been 75 years after the horrendous incident!

"Two generations survived and this is the third!" he said as he sat with his palm on his head as in deep thinking.

No! not again! Shouted Dr Davis teary eyed, in dismay as he reminisced.

****

Angela, his wife was expecting her second child. She was into her eighth week when all hell had broken loose. Every scan that Dr Davis did had only reconfirmed his findings of a mentally disabled child being born as they watched helplessly the turn of events.

Abortion de jure is illegal in Japan and so no chance of taking out the fetus! Both of them were terribly shaken

Every moment, every day and every month was turning into a traumatic emotional tumultuous roller coaster ride. Little Agatha would amble into the room talking gibberish and asking why her parents were crying even when her little brother was to arrive.
She was just five and was not able to decipher the meaning of the holocaust that had struck.
Little Jamy was born after a difficult caesarean section. He had a small head and all the sense organs seemed to be tucked in an odd fashion on his face. He looked abnormally frightening.

As days turned into years, Jamie was predictably slow on his milestones. He was diagnosed as a mixture of cerebral palsy and autism and was not able to grasp anything said or done. The doctors had pronounced after effects of radiation as the sole factor and there was nothing more to be done than helplessly watching Jamy moving towards deterioration each day.
****

The department of genetics was buzzing with activity today. Ten years of hard work had brought in results. Genome sequencing could show the new translocations on genes which now could be carefully and cleverly deleted by newer techniques.

Dr Anthony, as he held the mic, was giving all credits to Dr David who was emotional and was heard saying emphatically

"Never again"

17

The Happiness Potion

The hospital beds were overburdened by a volley of patients. Numerous tubes and beeping machines were hooked on to patients who looked sick and pale. The demography showed an interesting data. The patients were mainly in their early twenties, from elite homes and mostly were single children left alone in the company of gadgets while their overbearing helicopter parents gave them everything which they did not even need. They had the best of clothes, books,food,and yearly vacations to costly places.

Dr Anniruddh Shukla and Dr Jacob Mathews were the topmost physicians looking after this new disease which had gripped the city. Strange as it seemed even the best brains were not able to decipher the cause. All the blood tests done were within normal limits. Every diagnostic Xray or even CT scan and MRI gave no clue to what the patients suffered from.

Every patient had a common symptom. All the worlds' best food, clothes or even pleasures were not bringing them happiness. Melancholy surrounded them and they were not able to find a meaning in life. They were suddenly left disinterested and disenchanted from the world.

Dr Narendra Bajpayee who was the Dean of the Medical College in the city was approached and an emergency meeting was called. Dr. Bajpayee was in his late fifties but looked very fit and young.

He was known to be the Holistic doctor who not only believed in

evidence-based medicine but was a champion of an 'all-inclusive treatment' of patients. His book 'Live Life to the Fullest' was a chartbuster of sorts which taught people that Life was for healthy eating for both the body and the Soul...a concept which was for the very first time being advocated by a scientific mind!

He visited the hospital and gave each and every inmate a small bottle with some fluid. He asked this to be taken early morning in the lap of nature and asked for a sapling to be planted following this. The children had to "adopt" an underprivileged child and tutor them for at least an hour. They had to feed the stray cows and other animals as also wash their own clothes.

The patients dutifully followed and Lo! began showing signs of recovery. They started to smile and even laugh and developed an irresistible desire to do something meaningful for the society.

"Unbelievable doctor !" The media was inquisitive to know what was in the bottle given which was now unanimously named

"The Happiness Potion"

Dr. Bajpayee smiled and said....."Water and only plain water.....Happiness comes from toil ,positive engagement and our interaction with mother nature which has been blacked out by today's modern digital world! Happiness comes from giving and making others happy !"

18

What's this Life if full of Care?

What's this life if full of care?

We have no time to stand and stare !

I was relaxing on a hammock by the sea side enjoying the beautiful breeze and the rising sun. Sea birds which frolicked around gave me a glimpse of happiness. I watched the sun grow in size and warmth......and this was probably the first time I was watching the sun ....I was filled with glee just like a child....and wanted to shout out to everyone around. My wife and my two beautiful children were sitting in the lawns of the beautiful palatial sea side resort that we checked into. We were here not on a vacation as everyone goes to.......but for me....my treatment.......to get me out of the work stress that I had been suffering from of late. Everything seemed just like yesterday and memories began rolling in my mind just like a film reel......................

I had been given the prestigious *Best Student of the Year* award by my Medical College. I had also been the youngest surgeon to have completed the target task of the International Surgeons' Brigade in my city. I was at the top of the world. Work always gave me the high. Time just began rolling in leaps and bounds. Soon I was the most sought after surgeon with an international degree. My hands had the magic touch in them. I almost started feeling like God. Marriage

and children followed but were like nonentities for me....a small punctuation mark in a big sentence. I remember leaving home for work while children were still in bed and coming home late to see them tucked off to bed again. Only I knew the real meaning of happiness.......I had name, fame and money. I could buy anything in the world today....After all I earned for my family whom I loved.......I never felt hungry.......... ....skipped meals for the more important pending work. The wife had a packed meal ready for me when I went outside, and would always ask me to stop, and take a break.....I would look scornfully at her and tell her that money and time have to be the first priorities in life not her food. Time passed and I started experiencing pangs of abdominal pain every now and then. I started having headaches and sleeplessness. The mornings used to be drab and dry and I often woke up with a heavy head. I knew it was something very trivial and would go off with some pills...But it only aggravated and started to take a toll on me. My wife anyhow coaxed me to see a physician and undergo tests. She also asked me to take my friend along .I gave in to her wishes and called up my friend Dr Sushant. He was staying in the outskirts of the city and had invited me often to visit his beautiful abode. I thought this would serve the purpose of taking him along and also visiting him. He had called me early morning and he was strict about the timings. I felt annoyed but nevertheless heeded as I needed him today. I reclined in my luxury car and asked the chauffer to take me to the place. When I reached Arogya Nagar, my friends' place, I almost felt like a visitor to Paradise.....my friend was doing yoga under the Banyan tree with some of his friends. I could hear cuckoo birds singing and the cool breeze of the Neem trees which almost forested the big yard touched my forehead as if asking me to dance to their swaying branches. I waited for my friend who showed no hurry to leave his preoccupation to either meet me or attend any phone call. After an impatient wait of about an hour, he came up to me apologising and quickly adding that he did this on purpose. He actually wanted me to sit patiently for the time spent and see the difference. I was almost going to give a piece of my mind to him for wasting one whole hour of my precious time when he came out with W. H. Davies' What is this life if full of care We have no time to stand and stare

No time to stand beneath the boughs,

And stare as long as sheep and cows: ....he was going on and on and I felt my anger melting away and going into an enchanted aura where there was peace, bliss and serenity everywhere...........

He said ...."Now did you understand anything?" I had tears rolling down my cheek.....yes I understood everything.....in the rat race of earning money and becoming big I was losing my own self. He took my hand and said "Let's go to the specialist" I was astonished when I heard myself muttering " No buddy....I know my ailment now...........I know the treatment too......Please book tickets for me .....I need a break......a break from the daily grind to wake up into a new morning with double energy and attitude to LIVE TODAY rather than wait to live some day......"

19

An Ode to the Domestic Help

Everyday waking up to see her chappals was a pleasure......A "darshan" like relief.A neatly kept pair of old worn out green chappals kept in the adjacent flat would assure me of her arrival each day. Her name was Tugri, an odd name to my ears.After asking her name many times I settled for a "TORI" and addressed her so.She must have been in her early nineteens but looked much younger.Plump,her face would look swollen and would wear a smile making it look bright and pleasant. Her hair was very long and thick much to my envy,which she would braid into a long thick plait.

The door bell would ring and as I would open the door ,she would swooosh past me in a blink of a second and it would take me some time to realise that its Tori who has arrived.If you arent careful,she would bump into you...as she wouldnt look up and walk...so engrossed would she be in her profession. She would straightaway walk to the ante room,take out the broom,sweep the floors,mop them ,wash the balconies,water my Tulsi plant and head into the kitchen to wash the utensils.

She would wash them and stack them in their respective places.She would never fail to include the "sansi" and the kitchen knives in her daily load of washing.

One day I realised that there was no washing soap ....I was a little hassled at how on earth could Tori wash the dishes without a soap? I almost laughed when I discovered a "liquid soap" bottle which she had managed to fish out from my kitchen chest.I was surprised and amused at the same time.Not once would she tell me about anything lacking ,or anything unavailable.She had a quick substitute for everything.

If I were cooking whilst she did her work, not once would I see her head turn to see or know what was cooking.No smell would deter her from her work which she would continue to do diligently. The room would be littered with items all over the table ,some of them even expensive,but I have never seen her eyes roving or calculating about what was our worth!

Sometimes I would call her early during a pooja,or call her late in the evening if we had a trip next morning.There she would be on the dot ,like a dedicated soldier ready to give her every bit.She also carried a cell phone through which she communicated and made it easy for us to give her instructions if any.She would hang milk bags,and water bottles at the door before we came home after a long trip.She would buy vegetables or flowers whenever we needed them and wouldnt even ask us even if the money we owed was overdue.

A true professional that she was she taught me lessons of Punctuality and dedication and taught me to love ones work.It doesn't need an MBA degree to learn the philosophy of focussed working and this was taught to me by my help Tori

Its three months now that she has gone back to her hometown to marry and settle.I wanted to hug her and wish her good luck but could only give her some money and say it in a few words as no words are enough to say what she meant to me.

Wish you good luck Tori.

20
The Holy Ganges

"Naman Sethi" announced the receptionist of the Patna Medical Centre as many patients waited to consult the doctor.

Naman entered the doctor's chamber, and saw him engrossed in his medical reports.

" Your LFT and KFT are absolutely normal, your blood sugar shows..........."

" Come straight to the point doc! Tell me about the biopsy" Naman cut him short

"Well, I'm sorry you have a Colo-rectal carcinoma..." the doctor sounded grim

"Ok how much time do I have?"

"May be 2 months or even lesser! Apart from treatment only Prayers can help"

" Please doc! You know I'm an atheist. Just give me the higher center's reference"

"Here, take this reference for the best hospital in Delhi. You should start as soon as possible and start the treatment"

Thanking him profusely, Naman left the hospital lost in thoughts. He went home and began packing. Calling the driver, he asked him to pick him up early morning the next day.

The drive towards Delhi by road was expected to be of around eighteen hours. Seated comfortably behind, with a story book, Naman awaited his journey to treatment. He was a businessman

who was very practical and did not believe in anything beyond materialism. To him the realm of after-birth, destiny, or rituals were redundant and it was only the present rat race which could get you anywhere.

His chain of thoughts was broken as the car screeched to a halt.

"Sir there is a breakdown it seems. I will have to look for a mechanic", said the driver. "We are just on the outskirts of Varanasi and I'm sure we will get help."

The weather was pleasant and it was still just ten in the morning. Naman decided to take a small stroll towards the city while the driver went to get help.

"Sahab.. Sahab.... want to do Ganga Darshan?" Several rickshaw pullers crowded around him, each trying to bargain for the ride.

"What Ganga Darshan? Isn't it just a river?"

"Sahab! You are lucky that you are visiting Varanasi, and Ganga ...The place of 'Moksha' or salvation. The Holy Ganges isn't just a river...she is our mother who forgives our sins, who liberates our Soul from the cycle of rebirths"

Naman believed it all to be too ridiculous, but nevertheless thought of killing time whilst his car got repaired.

They travelled through narrow alleys; finally the ghats with steps leading to the pure Ganges was visible. Hundreds of thousands of pilgrims flocked to get a darshan or take a dip. Clanking of bells, chanting of mantras and the fragrance of incense sticks was melting Naman as he unknowingly started walking the steps.

Oh Ganga ! I come here to you as an orphan

O Ganga ! I come to you as a child

The 'Ganga Lahiri" was synchronizing with Naman's spontaneous dip into the river which were washing away his tears of ignorance.

The Holy Ganges had enlightened another Soul.

21
The New Normal

Mrs Agrawal is tired looking at her grey tresses, untidy eyebrows , blemishes on the skin and facial hair !

"How ! oh how I wish I could have learnt those beauty skills.I cant even hide my face behind those masks on a virtual kitty meet .....and I'm sure Mrs Bhalla with her eagle eyes would find out all my flaws" she was wailing...

Mauli was ransacking her cupboard....

" Gosh ! today is my presentation...and where did I keep those matching pants?"...

Mrs Chatterjee consoled her daughter..." never mind...wear your gathered skirts instead my girl !! You aren't visible below your 2nd button...

Haha Haha....." and they both laughed together..

Mrs Chopra is missing her percussion talent on the dholak which used to be lauded at every ladies' sangeet...

And she's suddenly taken aback by a phone call....

" Sudha....my daughters marriage has been fixed .Its going to be in the end of this month.We had to hurry as her would be uncle in law isnt too well...We' ll be having a virtual celebration ...and you have to be there virtually with the dholak..."

And Mrs Chopra started doing a bhangra..at home ...of course...

Siddharth and his gang of friends yearn for those pub nights...

Night curfews are still on and there isnt going to be a respite soon....

They decide to paint the town red...virtually....

They hold a zoom meet....guitar chords are strummed ...They have a riot eating and dancing....all in their own homes...yet together virtually...

"Doctor ....doctor..."....the ailing Mr Sinha coughs away while he's on a con call with Dr Awasthi..

Dr Awasthi advises him nebulisation and even shows how it can be done...he prescribes medicines and assures all would be well...

Suchita and Aman have their online school going on well.One click and they're at school......recess gives them time to nibble on to hot and fresh food....

Another click and school's over !

Mom also finds it easier now....no more getting up early in the cold to make and pack their breakfast....no more picking up and dropping.. ...so no more driving to and fro....

Mr And Mrs Singh have to work from home. They opt to move out from the metro to their native village...its better to be with family and why pay unnecessary rent?

Mrs Thakur is now a favourite Online customer...she WhatsApps s her local Kirana man her requirements and Voila !! The groceries reach her doorstep.She makes a quick online payment and is relieved...

Ms Sally hasn't bought her new make up kit since the last one got exhausted !! She dosent need one she says...

" The mask and the eye glasses are my saviours...she laughs away....no lipstick...no compact....no rouge....no eyeliners...no mascara...hahahaha....she cant believe she is living without makeup !

Welcome to the new normal!

22
Where Eagles Dare

Swati was on cloud 9.She had successfully completed her graduation and was looking forward to green pastures.

She had always wanted to join the Indian army and serve the Motherland.

She was mocked many a times by her peer and even relatives.

"What will you do in the army? You are a girl...you won't be able to stand the tough conditions..."

Though Women had been allowed to join the Army there were no areas for women combat officers till BSF allowed women to join in 2013.

She appeared for the CDS (Combined Defence Services) examination and was inducted as a probationary commandant .Rigorous training followed and it wasn't easy.Specially those five days on which women require rest were the toughest.

Further she had to face a lot of sexual discrimination in a male dominated field.She was the target of many sexist jokes which she gulped as part of a professional hazard which she had taken by choice.

Her hard work and determination bore fruit when she successfully completed her training with flying Colours and was posted in the tough terrains of the Country along with men who thought she was inferior.

Suddenly there was news of enemy attack on borders. The contingent she was leading was fully prepared for any combat operation.But her immediate senior was a little sceptical.He wanted to send her junior to the battle field .She was livid and her love for the Motherland along with her grit and determination forced the senior to take back his orders.

She was the commander in charge and led the troups towards successful elimination of the enemy .

****

Today is 15th August and she was being honoured with another medal to be decorated on her shoulder.

She smiled and stood with pride to recieve the honour from the Chief of the defence services who was heard saying...

"She flew where eagles dare."

...and there was a thundering applause....

Jai Hind...

23
Letter from Shanghai

♡

Year 2014

"You would be paid well for the procedure"; The infertility specialist was counselling Asha who had consented to be the surrogate for infertile couple. After a number of failed IVFs, James Antony and wife Chelsea had flown to India under medical tourism. An expat from France, they had been residing in Shanghai for the past three years. They had been hopeful this time, as Dr Neerja was one of the best specialists. After a quick battery of blood tests and scanning, Asha was given some injections to prepare her to conceive. James and Chelsea heaved a sigh of relief when the news of a successful implantation was received. Now it was only a matter of nine months and the bundle of joy would be in their arms!

"I just can't wait to hold her and cuddle her"...Chelsea was already on the seventh cloud.

The couple made their return plans, once the pregnancy test was positive. They were to return for the baby a week before the expected due date, and complete the formalities as per the Indian surrogacy laws.

****

Asha was being looked after well by the doctors and her staff as she regularly came for her checkups. Days turned into weeks and then months. The second ultrasound scan at around 13 weeks confirmed a twin pregnancy. When the intended couple in Shanghai were

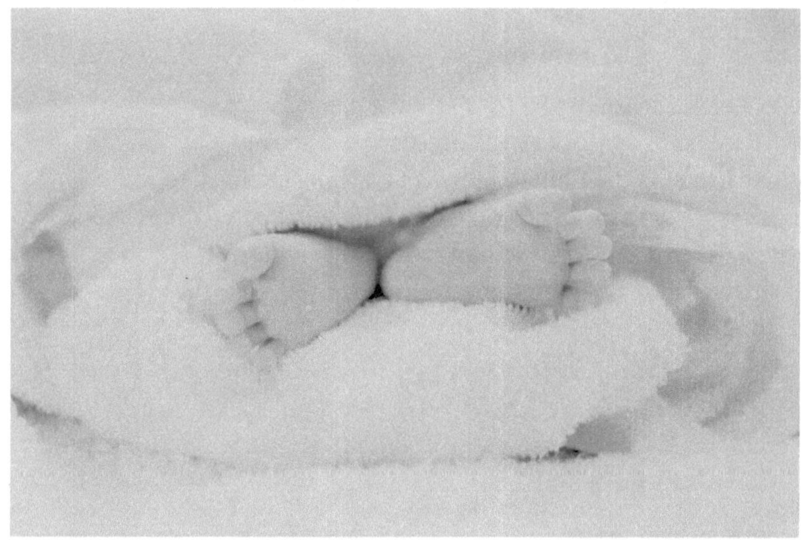

given the news, they were aghast. The joy of getting the baby was marred by angst and gloom as China had a strict one-child-norm failing which, the person could lose his job and even be jailed. They were in a dilemma, as they had no choice but to leave one child back in India, with the surrogate mother. With much desolation, they came to India a week before the due date. As planned the twins, a boy and a girl, were delivered by caesarean section. The surrogate mother who already had three children of her own was asked to keep the girl child and was paid extra money. The Couple also promised to take care of all her education and well-being. They took the baby boy and with mixed emotions flew back to Shanghai.

****

Year 2021

It was the 7th birthday of Julie as they had christened her before going back. Asha was busy decorating the house with balloons and festoons. She had even got a chocolate cake with *Julie* written on the icing. Her other three children enjoyed playing with Julie's curls and awing at her blue eyes.

"Post man" .... announced Kashiram ......" There is a letter from you from 'Phoren'

"What? for me? from 'phoren'? Deva re deva" .....muttered Asha

"Kaka...Please read it for me".. she pleaded......

Kashiram was reading the letter from Shanghai....

Dear Asha, As the Chinese norms have now changed to two children policy, we are coming to take our Julie back. We cannot thank you enough for taking care of her.

Asha was in tears of both joy and sorrow.

24

Lockdown–A Love Story

The session was over and results were awaited.

Anant and Shruti were excited as not only were they completing their MBBS and would be addressed as doctors but also that they would be soon entering into a wedlock.

Everyday efforts to enquire the University was becoming futile. They were becoming impatient as Only after the results could Anant go back to his home town Jabalpur.

Shruti was a resident of Delhi where she had done her schooling.

Hurray!......shouted Anant as he held some paper in his hands...

Dr Shruti! You have topped the list!

Whoa ..Dr Anant.....Shruti Chuckled...what about you?

I'm there too...but do not figure in the top 3...he said with a made-up disappointment on his face...

Both of them gave their customary HI five to each other and started talking about future plans...

"Put on the TV Anant"....said Shruti..."The Virus is gripping China and I'm afraid it would soon land here..."

News was flooded with the same depressing news of disease, deaths and fear.

They shut it off and started packing.

Tickets had already been booked by flights and they had decided that the marriage would be held in Delhi, Shruti's hometown.

Covid 19 cases had started raising their dirty heads everywhere...across countries....

In about 3 - 4 days.... things drastically started to change.

Covid 19 was taking its toll...All countries were being affected.... A pandemic had been declared....and the only remedy was a lockdown...

Lockdown?...Shruti was uncontrollable.... sobbing she asked her dad what it actually meant...

Her dad pacified her and told her it was a matter of just some weeks.

There Anant registered himself for voluntary services with other doctors and decided to serve mankind in this time of grave need.

"Have you gone mad Anant? You are just an MBBS...what will you do there? and our life hasn't even started."...shruti cried...

Anant was determined...."Shruti...calm down dear....nothing will happen to me....and I have my protective gear on....We HAVE to curb the rising of this virus...it will only happen if we treat it on a war footing"

"I want to be there too...with you....in every step".....said Shruti....helplessly...knowing well that a lockdown banned any kind of travel...

Every day was like an eon....and each evening she would impatiently wait for Anant's call and pray for him..

****

Six months passed...

The cases of Covid started to show a decline...

There were more cures and milder infections.

Anant was relieved of his duties and was felicitated by the Chief Minister.

Shruti declared. . the marriage would be held not in Delhi....her home...but in Jabalpur Anant's home...

Shehnai and other instruments played.... while Shruti and Anant tied the knot...

And both of them said together...

We had already locked our hearts together....

How could a lockdown separate us?......and the giggles and laughter echoed.....for years....

25

The Reunion

The school reunion had been arranged in Delhi. The class mates from Yashodhara Public School were going to meet for the first time after 10 years.

I was particularly excited, as I had established myself as a successful entrepreneur enjoying worldly pleasures. I owned a jaguar, a palatial house, was on foreign trips and was high on life.

Arun, Shiva, palash and I-Sudeep, were bosom buddies.... Though the 3 of us had been in touch, Arun was never found on social media.

We had recently got his phone number from another junior from school, and had given him a call requesting him to come for the reunion...He did not sound very happy or even pleased to talk to us. Upon insistence he reluctantly told us his address in Delhi and had hung up.

But his behaviour was upsetting...what arrogance!! What pride!!!

Palash and Shiva suggested that we should definitely meet him and show that we are no less...we weren't toppers but still have made a name for ourselves. The school rivalry would surely be forgotten as a silly past now as we were all in the same social status in life now.

Palash was establishing himself as a lawyer and Shiva had finished his MBA and was in a good job.

Arun had been the school topper throughout.

He was the only one from our close friends, to qualify for IIT, and his American dreams had been realised. After he left, we had lost

touch with him and it was only now that we could get to know his whereabouts. We were thrilled to know that he was in Delhi......

I wanted to meet him and all others. I wanted to know what they were doing in life.

Oh! how exciting everything was looking.

I suddenly went back in time reminiscing on my school days.......

****

Every day at school was becoming a nightmare. As I was not very good at studies, every teacher had loads of complaints against me. Look at Arun!

Look at his copy books... Look at his hand writing.

Look at his project...

Oh God I was sick and tired of this comparison.

Shiva and Palash, my friends were also equally reprimanded.

Arun's life had become a mark churning machine. He was more interested in getting his scores changed if he lost even half a mark. Gradually he was becoming more and more arrogant, looking down upon other children who did not score well. There would be a queue to borrow his notes and he would make many excuses before

lending them. Sometimes he would give it with contempt,
" what will you do with my notes? It's not the notes...it's the grey matter which matters."

Every annual examination had his scores high in flying colours. He had maintained, he wanted to be in a premiere institute like IIT and leave India for good.

"I wish to go abroad and pursue my studies there", he would boast.

"What about you?" He would scorn at me....

"You can never crack big exams buddy. Just do not even try them. Be happy taking up any sundry job in this small town".

Days and months turned into annual academic years and we soon saw ourselves reaching the 12th class. This year was an important landmark as we all were set to give our 12th board exams. "This year is your deciding factor, students!" Our principal Mr. Shukla was addressing us before the exams. "Prepare well and you'll have no regrets".

He had a special liking for Arun. He smilingly looked at him, ruffling his hair.

So Arun! All well son?

"Yes sir!" replied Arun, confidence oozing out.

"I have great expectations from you son and I know you would live up to our expectations"

As expected, Arun had not only topped the school but had cracked many examinations including the IIT.

****

In the evening we set off to Arun's house navigating with our Google map.

We had thought of paying him a visit before the main event, inviting him formally for the same.

As we adjusted our ties and tuxedos, we rang the doorbell.

A young lady opened the door and asked who we were. When we told her we were Arun's classmates, she ushered us in and offered us chairs in the living room.

Then she went inside and came back

.

wheeling Arun on a wheel chair....

..

We were shell shocked....

What. had...happened...to Arun....?

He had lost both his legs to an accident while in America and had to come back home.

As soon as he saw us, he started crying loudly like a child....

We were in tears ...as we were listening to Arun saying...

"Life is the biggest exam....not board exams...not entrance exams....

Gear yourselves up to face life....

I never enjoyed the small joys in life. I never made friends with you all thinking that I was supreme because of my high scores.

Exams and marks are mere numbers which do not help you in facing the ups and downs of real life...Academically good also means becoming a good human being first."

..

I found all my anger towards Arun melting...I found my tie and the tuxedo teasing me...The Jaguar like a dwarf....as I thanked God for keeping me healthy and alive.

26
Charity (nano-tale)

She was distributing masks as part of an NGO. They were the costliest and the most protective. Photos were taken and uploaded on the net. She was overwhelmed with the likes and comments she got. Her job was over.

He was wrinkled and old. Shabbily dressed with a painful hump back he was collecting all the used masks littered on the ground. His gloves were torn and he was picking dirty stuff with barren hands.

After all, cleaning the environment was the sanitation worker's sole responsibility without anyone even knowing!

27

Mother's Day (nano-tale)

❦

He drove down to the old age home in the next street. His mother had been waiting for him as he visited only on Mothers' Day. Teary eyed she hugged him, blessed him while he handed over his mobile phone to the chowkidar to click pictures.

He cut a cake, hugged his mom, smiled and laughed and left.... till he would return next year.

He updated his profile picture with the caption **'God could not be present everywhere so he made**

Mothers ...'

Love you mom.

HAPPY
Mo
HAPPY
mother's
DAY

28
A Memorable Train Journey

Bhola and Lakshmi had got their railway tickets booked in the sleeper class. It was after five years that they were going home to celebrate chatth Pooja in their home town in Bihar with their family.

With little Pooja in her arms, Lakshmi climbed up the stairs of the train compartment with aching arms and a bleeding heart with Bhola lugging in an old suitcase and a tattered kit bag from behind her.

As they both figured out their seats, they tried to settle themselves looking forward to meeting their family the next day.

Lakshmi's eyes had become dry and sore after that dastardly incident five years ago. Not a day passed without crying.

****

How happily they had gone to the fair in Ghaziabad where Bhola had got a new job in a garment factory. Sumit, their six-year-old son was insisting on going on the giant wheel.

As they bought tickets for the ride, and were about to enter the gate, there was a ruckus and loud voices. A gunshot was heard and people started running hither and thither. Little Sumit pulled his fingers off Lakshmi's hand in the melee' that followed and disappeared in the darkness. Distraught Bhola and Lakshmi ran around looking for Sumit but every one seemed to be running

aimlessly to save his life.

The police station was already choked with people who were bleeding, gasping, crying, shouting after the fracas that had ensued. Somehow Sumit's missing complaint could be lodged with difficulty.

Days and months with no news of Sumit. Both Bhola and Lakshmi were inconsolable but surrendered to fate.

Four years passed and Lakshmi gave birth to Pooja. Even if they say time heals it could not for the couple.

"If he had died that day we would've accepted the bad fate....but where did he go suddenly?" Bhola would cry often

The train whistled and started chugging.

Chai Chai.....Pakode......cutlet.......the vendors were busy

A boy in tatters almost smeared in soot and grease came in ....'shoe polish......shoe polish .....'

Maa ji......ma ji......shoe polish

Lakshmi looked at him.........and started shouting

Sumit.......my sumit........my Bablu..........

Bhola came down from the upper berth and before he could understand, he saw Lakshmi holding the boy close and throwing rapid-fire questions.

Sumit shared that he remembered being separated from his family during a shootout in a town. He was carried away by a group of angry mob and dumped elsewhere. A cobbler took him home, and fed him after making him labour for the whole day.He taught him the trade and now its been a year that he travels in trains.

Lakshmi showed him her picture holding him when he was six.

They got down in the next station, with Sumit, and headed straight to the police station to claim custody on their lost son who had been found.

They all cried and mentioned 'what a memorable train journey this!'

29

Until Death do us Part

As Isha was waiting for her turn in the chemotherapy unit of the Cancer hospital, Dhruv, her husband was holding her hand and constantly pepping her up.

It's nothing. Just see how you come out fit and fine..

And don't you remember?. You cannot go now...we have a long life to live together...

Here! take this marriage picture of ours.. and think of those beautiful days..........he was going on and on to boost her

While Isha reminisced...

Married at an early 21, she was very beautiful ,with long curly tresses ..

Dhruv was a simpleton and could never match her dressing sense.. and how irritated she would become when he dressed up shabbily for parties.

As time flew.. she became more beautiful and vain. Dhruv started having a receding hairline and even developed a paunch..

Ufff Dhruv! can't you do something?

Just look at you...My friends have started laughing at me because of you....

Poor Dhruv would just laugh it away and say...Oh my beautiful princess...you are so charming ..

That fateful day brought in a bombshell when she was diagnosed with cancer. A radical surgery of the breast made her confidence

shatter over losing feminine attributes that she boasted of. The following chemo sessions made her bald...the hair, the curls...

oh my God...

She couldn't look in the mirror... and threw a pen at it to shatter the glass.

Dhruv entered...and embraced her, wiping her tears...

Holding her close...he was saying...who needs those so-called womanly features?

We are Soulmates...and I am still your biggest admirer....my Princess....as he went on his knees to present to her a beautiful rose.... he started repeating the wedding wows...

Until death do us part.

Isha was crying incessantly...asking for forgiveness.

30
My World of Fantasy

It was all happening like a dream. Asha was getting married to Amar in a quick celebration. They had met each other on a dating site and had clicked off from the word go. Asha was an architect and had obtained some projects adding to her experience.

Amar was a techno geek, working for a giant company. He appeared to be a happy-go-lucky person smiling and laughing.

The arrangements for the wedding were superb and every event made memorable by video recording.

As the couple were heading to the airport to go to Delhi where Amar worked, suddenly Amar remembered he had forgotten to take his important tote bag. The driver was instructed to return and a visibly disturbed Amar raced into his bedroom looking for his bag. Amar could be seen sweating as he searched everywhere.

"Here! is this what you're looking for?" smiled Asha as she handed him a blue bag.

Amar almost snatched it from her much to her annoyance.

They then resumed their onward journey.

****

"Good morning, Amar" Asha came in with two cups of coffee

Amar smiled and taking a cup said, "hope you are getting used to life here! The maids are difficult to get and we need to do so much work ourselves. He was now and then holding on to the blue tote bag which he had painstakingly got.

Asha was getting curious to know what was in that bag and before she playfully tried to take it from him, he hid it behind the shelf and dodged Asha while she left sulking.

She was determined to figure out what's in that bag which even she was kept blind to.

****

That night Asha couldn't sleep. She was tossing and turning on bed. Suddenly she saw Amar getting up from bed. She dismissed it thinking he has gone to the wash room and kept lying down pretending to sleep. But when after quite some time, Amar didn't return, she followed him softly walking towards the wash room. She saw the small anteroom lit up surprisingly. Wanting to switch off the lights as she walked in, she had shivers.

It was a play room of sorts. Toys were strewn all over the floor. That same blue tote bag was waide open with stuffed toys coming out.

Amar was in his pajamas talking to the teddies, laughing and cooing and cajoling them. Asha called out almost shouting

Amar what's all this?

And to her dismay he started crying, throwing a tantrum!

Asha quickly called the family doctor online. He calmed her and explained that Amar was suffering from *FPP (fantasy prone personality) disorder.* Probably in his childhood, his busy parents pushed him into believing that these toys are alive.

Asha and Amar are both now going to a psychologist for counselling sessions and he has assured them complete freedom from this disorder.

* 9 7 9 8 8 8 5 5 5 6 7 9 8 *